Ruby
to the Rescue

MAGGIE GLEN

G. P. PUTNAM'S SONS   *New York*

For Calum and other little bears who hate being washed.
Also for Marie and Caroline, with thanks for all their help.

First American Edition published in 1992 by
G.P. Putnam's Sons, a division of The Putnam & Grosset Group,
200 Madison Avenue, New York, NY 10016.
Originally published in 1992 by Hutchinson
Children's Books, London
Printed in Hong Kong
Typography by Kathleen Westray.
Library of Congress Cataloging-in-Publication Data
Glen, Maggie.
Ruby to the rescue / by Maggie Glen.
—1st American ed.   p.   cm.
Summary: Ruby the teddy bear is taken to school by
her owner and carries out a plan to save two unwanted teddies
in the playhouse there.
[1. Teddy bears—Fiction.] I. Title PZ7.G48285Rv 1992
[E]—dc20   91-18991   CIP   AC
ISBN 0-399-22149-2
1 3 5 7 9 10 8 6 4 2
First Impression

*T*oday's the day, thought Ruby. I can't wait to see what school is like…

Ruby had heard a lot about school from Susie. At last she was going to see for herself. Mom waved goodbye, and Ruby and Susie set off with Grandfather.

At school, Susie left Ruby in the playhouse with the other toys who lived there. They stared at Ruby and pointed.

"You're funny-looking," said a big bear with a torn ear.

"I'm Ruby and I'm special," Ruby said firmly.
"Who are you?"

"I'm Big Bear," he said, putting his arm
around a small bear. "And this is Small Bear.
We're Anyone's Bears."

"What does that mean?" Ruby asked.

Before they could answer, the door to the playhouse opened and two children rushed in. They both grabbed Big Bear.

"I want the big bear today!" the boy said.

"No, he's mine!" shouted the girl. "I saw him first."

They tugged and tore at Big Bear. Ruby growled, but they didn't hear her.

"Stop this," the teacher said, looking into the playhouse. "The bears are for everyone. They're anyone's bears. You have to share them. No wonder the bears get so torn and dirty."

"Phew! That was no fun!" said Big Bear, when the children had gone.
"You've got another hole," said Small Bear.
"And I thought school was supposed to be fun," Ruby muttered.

Just then they heard the teacher talking to the children.
"The toys are very dirty again. Should we give them a bath?"
"Yes!" the children shouted.
"Oh no," Big Bear groaned. "That's the worst thing that could happen."
"I was soggy for a week last time," said Small Bear.

"Quick, under here," whispered Ruby, as they heard the children coming toward the playhouse.

The bears and Ruby dived under an old curtain in the dressing-up box. Ruby and the bears didn't make a sound while the children picked up the toys for a bath.

"I can't stand much more soapy water, or any more holes," groaned Big Bear. "What are we going to do?"

"Well, it's no good staying here where the children don't look after you," said Ruby. "You need to be with someone who thinks you're special."

"Us? Special?" said Small Bear.

"All bears are special," Ruby answered.

"Don't be silly," said Big Bear gruffly. "We're so dirty and full of holes, who would want us?"

"Someone will!" said Ruby. "Just let me think."

"I've got it," she said suddenly.
"Got what?" the bears asked.
"An idea," Ruby whispered. "Follow me."

While the children were busy washing, the three bears tiptoed out of the room. They crept down the corridor to the school door just as fast as they could go.

When they got outside, Ruby stopped.

"Wait here by the trash cans," she said, "and don't worry, I'm sure my idea will work."

Then she said goodbye and ran back inside.

The two bears looked at each other.

"We're on our own now," whispered Big Bear. "I hope she's right."

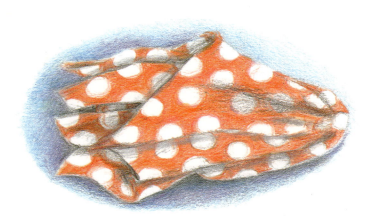

The bears waited and waited. Suddenly they heard loud banging noises.
"I'm scared," whispered Small Bear.
"I'll look after you," said Big Bear.
They heard a big deep voice booming down at them: "Look at these little fellas, Tom. They're about ready for the trash."
"You're right, Bill," said another loud voice. "They look as if they've had a hard time."

Bill lifted Anyone's Bears gently. Then the men began to smile.
"Looks like this one needs a bandage," said Tom, pointing
to Big Bear's ear.
"He could use some sewing up, too," said Tom.
"I think they like us," Small Bear whispered.
Bill laughed. "This little bear's got a squeaker."

Bill put Anyone's Bears in the cab.
"From now on you ride with us," he said.
The rabbit in the corner smiled.

A whole week went by. At last it was trash day again. Ruby watched from Susie's bedroom window. She crossed her paws and hoped her idea had worked.

At last the truck pulled up outside Ruby's house. And there, right up front in the cab, sat Anyone's Bears.

Ruby jumped up and down and called out, "Hello there!"

They looked up and saw her waving.

"Hey, Ruby, look at me," cried Big Bear. "I'm special now."

"Me too!" shouted Small Bear.

Ruby grinned at the two happy bears. "Of course you're special," she said. "Just like me."